Stuff wot I rote

2022

Trudy Bovey

*I hope you enjoy this wandering of my
brain. With thanks xxx*

Contents

The Monster

The Monster that lived in the tower
had known for a number of years
that the reason for its existence
was to prey on the folly of fears
was to act out the greatest of evils
was to bring down despair, loss and pain
That was, after all, its experience
and so, it enacted the same
In its own contemplation of living
it had come to a terrible place
where the thought of continuing on
bought it nothing but dread and disgrace
and deciding to end its own story
to the highest rampart was bound
and down from the uppermost parapet
the monster dropped hard to the ground
On waking, a sight unexpected
Not dead, but held, gently and sweet
with the tears of an innocent maiden
In a shock - the beasts heart skipped a beat
With assurances gentle and kindly
was bade rest and recover full health

It appeared that this saviour was willing and kind
her heart a most valuable wealth
After sleeping, and eating and resting
the monster arose from its bed
and when the maiden returned to its side
It kissed her, then bit off her head.

Revenge on the Unseen

She hatched a plan to get her revenge
on the children that lived next door.
Their screaming and crying was awful.
She knew how to teach them for sure.
Although usually eye-contact avoiding
she engaged with the mother one day
They had never really spoken
but she knew what she wanted to say
"My sister's kids are visiting
I thought I'd take them to the zoo
and I was just, wondering if,
your girls would like to come too?"
The Sun came out in the household
How kind, what a lovely thought.
The girls are dressed and sat ready
and that is how they were caught.
She did have her niece and nephew
She did take them out to the zoo
But she 'totally forgot' about the neighbours,
"Oh dear, well, what can you do..."
She smiled to herself in contentment
But really, what did she achieve?
The crying and banging continued.

That, the plan did nothing to relieve.
It successfully hurt further two children
Who's abuse happened every day.
Who did not understand, the iron hand
that filled their life with pain.
Who had thought, for the first time ever,
that there might be some kindness out there,
that the world outside their small circle
might contain other people who care
But as they waited in silence
at first happy, excited and keen
the hour ticked by
and they never knew why
they were left behind unseen.
The endless fear to continue
the physical punching and more
The inconvenient screaming
of the two little girls next door.

I Confess

I did it, I definitely did it
I admit it, I know it was me
For years I have had to live with it
But I really want to be free.
At the time I thought it was funny
A friendly. amicable jest
an amusement, that's all
but when I recall
it was really not me at my best
I hope you can forgive me
I hope it did no lasting harm
I have always carried it with me
and it still disturbs my calm
It sits among some others
that easily come to mind
My failures and my blunders
and the Me's I've left behind.
I don't know if I will ever
forget, but maybe I've learned
So, I wanted to write you this message
In case you ever returned.

Hurting

Did you know I have had my heart broken?
Did that ever happen to you?
Did you yearn in vain unspoken?
or had your insides ripped in two?
Have you sobbed into the carpet,
been stunned into deepest despair?
Ah, I see I've hit a sore spot
there is something of you also there.
Well perhaps there is something in sharing
Perhaps, although painful, its true
It helps me to know that you've been there
and that both of us have made it through.

Relax

And now a return to breathing
and now a return to now
My ears are fully hearing
relaxing, I allow
A return again to breathing
Allow my thoughts to go by
no judgement on their leaving
I melt away the I
No thoughts are now required
No observations come
Instead, a gentle feeling
of everything as one

And then a return to breathing

Poetry stops sleep

FFS will you stop it
this poetry on tap
It isn't funny anymore
I bet the next one's crap
What do you think you're doing
Just saying things like that
I bet when you look back on this
you'll wish you'd shut your trap
I'm serious about this
it's like some sort of curse
You cannot think a single thing
that doesn't come in verse
You'll have to exorcise it
get it out of your head
You can't have poems going round
ambushing you in bed

Fat Ball Limerick

The Robin came a bobbin
The Sparrows arrived in a mob
The two Bluetits slid down the poles
and the Blackbird barged in with a squab
The feeding dish was busy
It always is that way
It will help them get through the winter
and it brightens up my day

Samantha

I first met Samantha in college
We shared classes, not socially
There was something that stood out about her
Something that, maybe she didn't see.

It was nothing that someone could point at
not an attribute noticed by eye
It was something more like a vibration
that I felt, when she was close by

When we once had occasion to natter,
I asked her if we had met before
But we could not find an occasion
so we spoke of it no more

We just talked about something and nothing
it was comfortable, friendly, too brief
And I felt this strange connection
was going on underneath

I couldn't quite understand it
when I talked about it with mum
she said; we were probably related
in a life past, or perhaps yet to come

I last saw Samantha in college

We never were close, way back then
Though I fondly remember her presence
and I feel like I'll meet her again

There are just certain people I notice
Like a long-lost friend again found
and it feels like there's just, some connection
Even when they're no longer around

The Old Harbourmaster's Cat

Loudly the wind was roaring
the swell was as high as a tree
when the boat broke free of its mooring
left the harbour
and into the sea

As the waves crashed over its decking
and the eddies turned this way and that
the only witness, and victim
was the old harbourmaster's cat

The boat had seemed such a comfort
when the cat sought retreat from the rain
Now its claws hung on to an awning
and the world span around in its brain

A catastrophe in the making
a huge wave bore the boat up high
the momentary stillness
was a storm with a cat in its eye

But, strange to any who saw it,
and only I saw it was so,
that the boat was let down in the harbour
and the wind, it ceased to blow

Now, I don't know for certain
for surely, no one can say,
If the cat, that sat, in the harbour
Had lost a life that day

But he's back with me now, by the fire
and the boat is fine, and that's that
It's a night we will always remember
The Harbour master and his cat.

Bye-Bye Now

I'll meet you again in heaven
I'll see you on the other side
and even if you don't believe in that
We'll find out when we've died.

See ya later alligator
Au-revoir for now my friend
It has been quite an experience
and I'm ready for it to end

Have peace. Live long and prosper
May all your wishes come true
I am off on my next adventure
Till we meet again, adieu

Understanding Myself

To understand my point of view
I'd have to describe it from viewpoint two
and, if I were - so to do,
I'd be describing it to who?
Well, that would be to viewpoint three
who then tries to explain to me
While watching out for viewpoint four
who's always trying to jam a foot in the door

So, one just does
and two reports it
three reviews
and four distorts it

The past and future are viewpoint four
misremembered and not for sure
Three has issues of its own
and doesn't always act full grown
two sleeps a lot
one acts with stealth
I'll never understand myself!

Now and Always

There is nothing I would not do for you
Lift your arms and feel my embrace
there is nowhere I cannot find you
I know you, I know your face

Just see me here in everything
We can never be apart
You and I, and all there ever was
belong to the one shared heart

You have senses and a mind to think
a way to reflect on the day
Do you see me there in the simple things
I am present in every way

I know that life is testing you
I know it is sometimes pain
Know all will pass and be made anew
and you will feel joyful again

Do not wait for me in the later on
I am here, and always now,
I love you unconditionally
Look inside, I will show you how

Distractions are multitudinous

Sensation is all around
Remember what really matters
and keep your feet on the ground

Be brave my love in the face of fear
Take heart in the love that you give
Be kind to all, and to yourself
Live the life only you can live

Give to others, as only you can
do the things only you can do
be the you that you are meant to be
and I will be loving you

When I was a kid, it was different

When I was a kid, it was different
I would be out from tea-time 'til night
Getting in that last adventure
before the failing light

I would swing really high in the playground
I'd go sneaking around in the trees
I'd be running all over the neighbourhood
Just doing whatever I pleased

Sometimes I'd play with my sister
Sometimes our friends were around
Sometimes I'd just wander off in the street
and see what else could be found

When I was a kid, it was different
The phone was attached to the wall
and if anyone wanted to find you
they would lean out the window and call

I would walk down the road to the churchyard
I'd go round to my friend's house for tea
I would hide from the rain in a bus stop

I was utterly, totally free

Sometimes I'd play in the wasteland
Sometimes I'd just run and run
When I got a bike, I'd go scrumping
Everything seemed like fun

At a summer camp in the city
there was no health and safety back then
All the kids were given a hammer and nails
and we couldn't have been more than ten

In the holidays we went fishing, and
I made my own camp, with fern weaving
I watched a snake as it shed its skin
and I fished from my bay 'til the evening

Sometimes we only had meat once a week
Sometimes we had beans on toast
but usually, every Sunday
we would all sit down to a roast

When I was a kid, it was different
Everyone watched the same show
So, when you got back together
You could talk about something you know

I would lay on my back in the sunshine
I would swing from a tyre on a tree
Throw stones in the air to attract a bat.
I'd play my tapes endlessly

Sometimes, when I remember
The freedom and things that I did

TRUDY BOVEY

I just can't help but think to myself
It was different when I was a kid

Hey MP getting money from Lobbyists

Excuse me, I think you've forgotten
I think you must have skipped a page
You do not seem to remember
it is we that pay your wage

So, you don't find that satisfactory
and you sub it from your mate
his business makes a donation
and ties itself to your fate

I'm sorry, but that cannot happen
so, you think that you need more and more
you must learn how to cut your cloth now
not try to keep up with next door

I know, you can't even imagine
What it means to live like we
To many, the things that you value
are not based in reality

We need you, in the right place
We need your word to be true
We need good vision and leadership

Can you tell me, is that you?

I am sure you are doing your best now
but don't wander too far by yourself
Just remember, you represent US
We're not a means for you to get wealth

Not Listening

There was something sad in her eyes that night
as she reached for the keyboard to type
the words seemed dull and meaningless
she was not living up to the hype

Nothing at all was different
Her output had not really changed
But she'd started to read and listen
to the whiners and the deranged

The night had come, and the moon was bright
and she stopped a while for a break,
but the criticism went on in her head
it was more than her soft heart could take

Why, she thought, should I even try
what point was there to going on
what right have I to put down these words
Where does it all come from

At last, so tired, she fell asleep
as her energy faded away
She gave her thanks as she always did
and hoped for a bright new day

When she awoke in the early light

the dewdrops were still glistening
She smiled and knew what the secret was
and she simple just stopped listening

Ha ha, said they, or even worse
It glanced off her without harm
For in her heart was a new resolve
and it worked for her like a charm

"So many brothers and sisters have I
and not one of them is the same
If they want to winge or criticise
then that shall be their fame

For me, I choose not to hear them,
unless it is helpful or kind
They cannot take what I do not give
By Not Listening, I leave them behind"

and so, she returned to her passion
not stopping to think or review
and I for one will join her
and I hope that you do too.

The Lady of Shallot

The tower held a lady fair
a witch's curse had placed her there
Upon the land she could not stare
The Lady of Shallot

Through jealousy her fate was sealed
her whereabout were not revealed
and memories of her concealed
a prison for her to rot

To Camelot she would never go
The Witches curse had made it so
Alone her life would pass more slow
The Lady of Shallot

A mirror served a job to do
To see outside she would look through
Reflections were her only view
and this she did a lot

She watched the river slipping by
distant Camelot held her eye
no-one came near to hear her cry
The lady of Shallot

The lady in her mirror gazed

as on the hillsides shepherds lazed
and crops were sown and cattle raised
and everyone forgot

She saw the seasons come and go
and soon there was no-one to know
that she had ever been, and so
she vowed to change her lot

The Lady in her mirror saw
someone she had not seen before
a Royal crest and helm he bore
but he could see her not

The thought of rescue hit her mind
She left her tower room behind
and down the stairs she quickly climbed
The Lady of Shallot

and to the riverside she fled
a boat she used to lay her head
and with the current it is said
she rode to Camelot

She wrote her name along the side
for now, she would no longer hide
although she neither could abide
The Lady of Shallot

She sang a song of deep lament
and everywhere the sad craft went
the ears of all to her were bent
though they did know her not

and there where reeds and willows weep
the water took her in final sleep
into the darkness and the deep
The Lady of Shallot

The Knight who gazed upon her form
so beautiful, yet so forlorn
Ordered her body to be borne
and laid in Camelot